Prologue:

The night hung heavy, thick with a suffocating silence. The moon cast its pale glow over the fractured remnants of a collapsed mountain, turning the rubble into jagged shadows that stretched across the land. Time had forgotten this place; the wreckage was a tomb for something far older and far more dangerous than the world had ever known.

But tonight, something stirred beneath the stone.

The earth trembled, faint but undeniable, as an arm with jagged claws broke through the rock. The ground groaned as she emerged from her prison, a head rising from the dark. The figure of a nightmare. The Mega Mosquito Queen had awoken.

Her once pristine hair, now longer and wild, cascaded like an inky green waterfall. Her tattered, ruined garments clung to her like remnants of a forgotten era. She had grown; evolved. Her body was a weapon now, every inch of her radiating an aura of brutal strength. Her claws, gleaming with lethal intent, stretched wide as she pulled herself from the rubble. Her eyes flickered with madness and hunger.

Behind her, a swarm of her Mega Mosquito Minions scuttled in frenzy, their screeches and howls filling the air. They followed her out of the hole she dug.

The final rocks were thrown aside, and she stood, stretching to her full height with her newfound muscles outlined beneath her ruined clothes. The cavern's faintly glowing crystals pulsed with energy: life-giving, power-infused energy that had kept her alive during her years of being trapped. She inhaled deeply, the air sharp in her nostrils, as her senses exploded. Every inch of her, every atom, was brimming with life.

Then, the memories came like a hammer strike to her skull. The defeat at the hands of Ry-tor. The bitter taste of that loss still burned in her mind. Her fists clenched, her claws digging into the stone beneath her. Her minions paused, sensing the shift in the air.

With a low growl, the Queen's voice slithered through the silence, venomous and twisted. "You won't escape me again..." Her words were a promise, cold and final. Her claws flexed in anger.

The minions, sensing their queen's fury, began to roar and screech, their wings buzzing with frantic energy. They knew their purpose: her will was their command. They were her army, ready to follow her to the ends of the earth and beyond.

She glanced at them for only a moment, a cruel, predatory smile curling at the corner of her lips. Without a word, she extended her wings, the leathery membranes stretching wide with a sickening crack. They unfurled, casting dark shadows over the wreck of her mountain. The Queen took a step forward, her feet digging into the earth as her wings flapped, sending gusts of wind swirling in every direction.

With a swift motion, she leaped into the air, her speed and agility more terrifying than ever before. The swarm of mosquito minions that had already gathered above her roared into life, a buzzing cloud of death and destruction. They moved with a mind of their own, streaking through the air like a living storm.

The Mega Mosquito Queen's eyes glinted with malice. She was a being of unrelenting force, speed, and anger. There was no one who could challenge her, not even *Ry-tor*. Her strength alone could shatter mountains, and her mind, sharp and calculating, would find a way to dismantle her enemies, one by one.

She watched as her minions shrieked and cried, echoing through the valley as they spread across the land below her.

"No one will stop my revenge on Ry-tor," she hissed, her voice a whisper against the howling wind.

And with that, the night swallowed her whole, her wings carrying her into the darkness. The terror had returned.

Part 1:

The morning sun poured down over the jungle, bathing it in golden light. The world was alive with the sounds of the wild: a chorus of birds calling out, the rustling of leaves in the wind, and the distant calls of unseen creatures deep in the jungle. But above it all, cutting through the breeze was the sound of wings.

Linwing soared high above the treetops, her mighty wings slicing through the air with an energy and grace that made the very atmosphere tremble. Every movement she made was deliberate and precise, a living embodiment of power. Linwing was made for the skies and carried with her a unique trait: the power to breathe fire.

Linwing's flames could burn with an intensity stronger than a dragon's fury. Her breath could scorch the earth, melt metal, and incinerate anything in its path. Despite the immense abilities she held within her, Linwing had made a promise to herself: she would never use her fire to hurt anyone or anything. Not if she could help it.

As she soared through the morning sky, her sharp eyes scanned the jungle below. Her eagle-like vision allowed her to see everything with perfect clarity. From high above, the world seemed peaceful. The trees swayed gently in the breeze, the leaves rustling with soft whispers. The jungle stretched out in all directions. It was the perfect view from the sky, the perfect peace.

And then, she saw him.

Beneath the towering trees, standing with all the majesty of a king in his realm, was Saborkris. The massive saber-toothed tiger looked up at the sky with his eyes gleaming in the sunlight. His brawny frame rippled with muscle as he shifted his weight on the ground. There was something noble about his presence, but there was also a warmth in his gaze that made him approachable and kind.

Linwing's heart swelled with affection as she flew through the air, her wings carrying her downward in a graceful arc.

"Morning, Linwing!" Saborkris's voice rumbled out in that deep, warm tone of his. It was the kind of voice that made everything feel alive, and Linwing smiled as she heard it.

"Morning, Saborkris!" Linwing replied, her voice light and teasing as she hovered above him. Her bright blue eyes sparkled with mischief as she took in his large, imposing form. "How's the jungle treating you today?"

Saborkris's gigantic tusks gleamed as he flashed her a toothy grin. "Better now that you're flying by. It's not every day I get to see my favorite parrot."

Linwing let out a loud, cawing laugh, the sound of it carrying through the air. Her feathers rustled as she tilted her head playfully. "Flatterer! Keep smiling like that, and I might get distracted and crash into a tree!"

Saborkris's amber eyes twinkled with humor as he shifted his weight, one huge paw resting on the dirt. "I'll catch you if you do," he said, his voice sincere and filled with affection.

Linwing's eyes twinkled in return, and she gave him a sly smile. "Oh, I'm sure you would." She fluttered her wings, sending a gust of wind swirling through the nearby trees. "But don't get too comfortable. I have something cool to show you today."

Without waiting for his response, Linwing shot upward, her wings fluttering with a powerful whoosh of air that sent a breeze rustling through the trees. Saborkris blinked, startled for a moment, before his eyes narrowed in determination. With a roar, he bounded after her, his enormous shape moving with the grace and speed of a jungle king.

Linwing flew ahead, the wind whistling in her feathers.

Saborkris, now just behind her, his muscles rippling beneath his sleek fur, bounded after her. Linwing's heart swelled with affection for him. He was more than just a friend - he was a constant presence in her life, a steady force of strength and warmth in an ever-changing world.

She hovered just above the treetops, looking down at him with a mischievous grin. "Come on, Saborkris! Keep up! We're almost there."

With that, she flapped her wings and shot forward like a streak of lightning.

Together, they explored the jungle. Linwing was full of surprises, and she was always ready for an adventure. Today would be no different.

Part 2:

Linwing and Saborkris made their way through the dense forest. Linwing's tail swished behind her, as she led the way, her feathers glistening.

"You know, I swear you know every inch of this place," Saborkris growled, though there was an affectionate tone in his voice. The huge saber-toothed tiger wasn't exactly the biggest fan of traveling through thick foliage, but he didn't mind as much when it meant hanging out with Linwing.

"Well, it helps that I'm not exactly restricted by, you know, legs," Linwing teased over her shoulder. She was on a mission today: to show Saborkris something that would hopefully make him laugh, or at the very least, relax. It was time for a break from the hustle of jungle life.

After weaving through the trees, they arrived at a hidden clearing; one that Saborkris had never seen before. In the center, a steaming hot spring sat nestled among rocks and lush greenery, the water shimmering with a warm, inviting glow. The gentle steam rising from the water made the whole area feel like a magical oasis.

"Whoa," Saborkris said, his voice brimming with curiosity. "What is this place? I've never seen anything like it."

Linwing grinned, her eyes sparkling with mischief. "It's a secret, Saborkris. You won't find this spot on any map. Well, except for my personal map. I mean, it's *my* secret spot, so, y'know... don't tell anyone!"

Saborkris squinted at the steam wafting from the water. "Uh, that water looks... hot."

Linwing giggled. "Not unless you're the weakest saber-tooth in the jungle."

Saborkris raised an eyebrow, letting out a low growl of amusement. "I'm not exactly a *water* kind of guy, Linwing. You know, fur, claws... It's not exactly ideal for swimming." He looked suspiciously at the bubbling water.

Linwing grinned mischievously. "Oh, you'll be fine. Think of it as a *joyful experience*." She then wiggled her wings in a little dance, as though to drive home how *fun* it was going to be. "Plus, it's *very* good for your fur. Makes it look all, um, shiny and smooth," she said with a wink.

Saborkris snorted again, still not convinced, but his curiosity got the better of him. He gingerly stretched a massive paw out toward the hot spring and dipped it into the water. The moment his foot made contact with the water, his eyes widened, and he pulled it back quickly with a surprised yelp.

"Whoa!" he shouted. "That's *really* hot!"

Linwing burst into a fit of giggles, clutching her sides as she watched the tiger's reaction. "I told you! But don't worry, it's like -" she hesitated, trying to find the right words. "It's like *hot tub hot*, not *lava hot*."

Saborkris gave her an incredulous look. "Hot tub? I'm a *saber-tooth*, not a *spa enthusiast!*"

Linwing couldn't contain her laughter. "I didn't say you were! But just imagine it, relaxing in here after a long day of hunting or roaring or whatever it is you do with all that *energy* of yours."

Saborkris sighed dramatically, shaking his head. "You're relentless, aren't you?"

Linwing's eyes twinkled as she shook her wings. "You bet I am!"

She soared through the air with ease, studying him keenly. Saborkris stood awkwardly at the edge of the spring, still not convinced about the whole water experience. Linwing, seeing her opportunity to make this a bit more fun, took a deep breath and, without warning, splashed a large wave of water directly at her friend.

"Whoops!" she said sweetly, though it was clear from the mischievous gleam in her eyes that she wasn't apologizing at all.

Saborkris yelped as the hot water splashed over him, drenching his fur. He shook his head furiously, spraying water in every direction, but his irritated expression slowly faded into a begrudging smile.

"You little…" Saborkris started, but before he could finish, Linwing shot up into the sky with a burst of speed that made the air around her crackle.

There was no warning, no time to prepare, just an explosion of motion as Linwing broke the sound barrier, her body becoming a streak of color as she rocketed into the heavens. The roar of her sonic boom rang out through the jungle, causing some nearby birds to scatter in panic.

"YEEHAW!" Linwing's voice echoed from above, her laughter ringing through the air as she tore through the sky playfully. "If you had wings, do you think you could catch me?" She shouted down to Saborkris, who was left standing in the steaming water, his fur soaked and his mouth hanging open in awe.

Saborkris blinked up at her, eyes full of admiration as he watched Linwing fly in a perfect loop, defying gravity with every twist and turn. And while he usually preferred the ground to the sky, he couldn't help but chuckle at the sight of his friend - *his parrot friend* - zooming around with such reckless abandon.

He let out a small snicker, his eyes softening as he watched her streak through the sky. "You're nuts, Linwing," he muttered with a grin, shaking his head. "But you sure know how to have fun."

"You're *nuts*!" Saborkris shouted again, laughing. Linwing's energy was infectious, and for the first time that day, he felt his usual gruffness melt away in the hot sun.

Linwing shot him a wink from above. "I'm always happy to go on an adventure with you, big guy!" She flew down and landed on a rock next to him. They had a fun day ahead of them.

SPLASH

SHAK
SHAK SHAK

Part 3: The Mega Mosquito Queen

The Queen stood tall in the shadow of the broken cave, surrounded by her Mega Mosquito Minions, her mind filled with twisted, calculated thoughts. She was no longer the weakened figure who had been trapped in that cave for years. The energy from the crystals - those mystical, shimmering powers that had been released when Ry-tor shot his lightning - had filled her with unimaginable strength. It was as if the world had opened up to her, offering her a new realm of possibilities. She had been reborn, and the world would soon know her name.

Her new look in her new clothes matched her newfound capabilities. Her wings, once delicate, were now thick and sturdy. They twitched restlessly behind her. They were ready to tear through the air and strike down any who dared to oppose her.

But there was something she needed; something more than just brute force. Something that would tip the scales in her favor. Revenge was her heart's desire, but it would require more than just physical strength. She had to be smarter, more strategic.

Ry-tor had wronged her. The lightning-wielding Velociraptor had been the one responsible for her downfall. He had shattered her perfect world and trapped her in the darkness. He was elusive, and no matter how many times she tried to track him, he always slipped through her grasp. The crystals had revived her, but now she needed more. She needed someone who could match Ry-tor's speed and intelligence. Someone who could help her catch him; someone with strength that could rival her own.

But the Queen had never heard of such a character. Until now...

A deep, guttural voice interrupted her thoughts. One of her minions emerged from the shadows and bowed low before her. "Queen, we have gathered information. There is a... a being. A force in the jungle. Something... or someone who might suit your needs."

The Queen's eyes flared. "Explain."

The Mega Mosquito Minion buzzed with excitement as it spoke, clearly eager to deliver this new piece of information. "A parrot of immense might and intellect, described as a flying beast with feathers like fire and a strength unmatched. They call her Linwing."

The name echoed in the Queen's mind, but it meant nothing to her. She had never heard of Linwing before. She didn't care about names. She cared about power. And this Linwing seemed to have plenty of it.

"Strength unmatched?" The Queen tilted her head, her thoughts already spinning a web of possibility. "Where is she? What can she do?"

The minion hesitated for a moment before responding. "She is known for her extraordinary flight, capable of reaching speeds faster than sound. Her physical strength rivals that of the mightiest warriors, and she can breathe fire of intense, scorching blasts capable of melting rock. She is nearly invincible, and her wings - they are deadly weapons.

The Queen's eyes gleamed with malice. This Linwing sounded like the perfect candidate. A creature with the ability to help her bring down Ry-tor. But she wasn't just going to ask for her help. No, she would manipulate Linwing into joining her cause. That was how the Queen worked; she used lies, deceit, and promises to make others see things her way. But this would require a careful approach. She couldn't rush it. If she played her cards right, Linwing would soon find herself caught in the web the Queen was spinning.

She stepped closer to the edge of the cliff, looking down into the jungle below. It was a vast, untamed wilderness; a place where a powerhouse like Linwing could hide, unseen, until it was too late. The Queen's thoughts grew darker and more focused. This was the moment she had been waiting for.

"Send out more scouts," the Queen ordered, her voice icy and commanding. "Find her. I need to know where she is, who she is, and how she operates."

The minions scattered, their bodies vanishing into the shadows, their wings buzzing with anticipation. The Queen remained, her eyes scanning the horizon; her thoughts continuing to churn.

She could see it already: the plan unfolding before her. Linwing's abilities were undeniable. She had the strength, the fire, and the speed necessary to be a formidable ally. And if the Queen was very careful, Linwing would fall into her trap without even realizing it.

She would make herself out to be a victim who had lost everything. The one who had been betrayed by Ry-tor. She would use Linwing's sense of justice against her with the promise of vengeance, of destroying Ry-tor, the Velociraptor. That would be the bait. The Queen smirked at the thought. Linwing would come to her. The parrot might not even realize what was happening until it was too late. She would offer her the chance to rule the kingdom, and in return, Linwing would fight by her side. Together, they could take down Ry-tor, and then, together, they would be unstoppable.

She looked over her shoulder, her minions still out there somewhere, gathering information and preparing to track Linwing down. The Queen was patient, and she knew that it wouldn't be long before the pieces of her plan would start to fall into place. In the meantime, she would wait. She would savor the anticipation. And when the time came, she would extend her offer to Linwing.

It would be a decision that could change everything.

The Mega Mosquito Queen stood there, her wings fluttering with anticipation, as the jungle continued to stretch out before her. A new chapter was about to begin.

Part 4: Linwing

Linwing looked at Saborkris with a playful smile. Her heart was light and content. Saborkris's bright eyes twinkled with fondness as he chuckled at her entrance. He shook his head, a grin spreading across his face. "You're always so good-humored and joyful," he said, his voice rich and deep. "That's what I like about you. You're always charging ahead, like nothing can stop you, whether it's your wings, or the fire in your heart. And even with all your incredible abilities, you never let it change who you are. You still laugh, still care about others. That is the stuff that makes you more than just strong. It makes you incredible."

Linwing's face softened, the playful look in her eyes giving way to a rare moment of tenderness. She stepped forward, lightly brushing her wing against his shoulder. "Thank you, Saborkris, for always being there for me, even when the world feels like it's going to swallow me whole. I'm not sure where I'd be without you."

There was a brief silence between them, one of those few times when both friends could just stand together and share the quiet peace of the jungle. Linwing's feathers shimmered in the golden light as Saborkris's deep, rumbling voice broke the stillness. "You're one of the few souls I know who can make even the darkest days feel like sunlight."

Linwing smiled, her eyes sparkling with warmth. "And you're the one who reminds me not to take things too seriously. Life's too short for that."

They exchanged a grin, the bond between them strong and unspoken. But their peaceful moment was soon shattered by an unexpected sound.

From deep within the trees came a rustling. The faintest crackle of branches. Linwing's sharp, eagle-like vision immediately snapped to attention, her body tense as she crouched slightly, wings half-spread, ready for anything. Saborkris, his senses amplified, growled low in his throat, his posture shifting into a more defensive stance.

The bushes parted, and from the shadows emerged a figure - a towering, imposing silhouette with leathery wings. A creature emerged, its eyes gleaming intensely.

Linwing squinted. "Who...who is that?"

Before she could finish her sentence, the figure stepped into the clearing, and the full extent of its form was revealed. The Mega Mosquito Queen stood before them, her minions buzzing around her like a swarm of vultures. The Queen's presence was like an oppressive weight in the air, her immense power practically radiating off her.

For a moment, no one spoke. Linwing and Saborkris exchanged a quick glance. They had never seen this creature before, but there was something unmistakably dangerous about her. Her eyes, wild and calculating.

"I... I need your help," the Mega Mosquito Queen said, her voice a low, gravelly rasp. There was an edge of desperation in her tone. "Please, I beg of you. I have been wronged by a terrible beast: a Velociraptor, a lightning-wielding menace. He's taken everything from me. You don't understand! I need to find him! I need to make him pay for what he did."

Linwing, ever the optimist, took a cautious step forward. "What happened? Who is this Velociraptor? Why does he need to be stopped?"

The Queen's eyes flashed, a flicker of emotion crossing her otherwise cold face. "His name is Ry-tor. He attacked me and destroyed everything I built. My kingdom, my strength... all gone. Please, I need your help. You have the ability to defeat him."

Linwing furrowed her brow, her curiosity piqued but her instincts still on edge. "Ry-tor? We've never heard of him. What makes you think we'd want to help you?"

The Queen's voice softened, a false sweetness creeping into her tone. "Because I know what it's like to lose everything. We're not so different, you and I. You've fought battles, haven't you? You know the cost of losing. This Ry-tor—he's dangerous. He's taken everything from me. If you join me, we can destroy him together. If we don't do anything now, he could destroy everything here, including you."

The mention of someone who had wronged her, someone who had hurt this Queen, resonated with Linwing in ways she didn't expect.

Saborkris, however, wasn't convinced. He stepped forward, his usually gentle eyes were hard, suspicious. "Linwing, be careful. We don't know anything about her. She could be lying. There's something off about her. We can't just rush in because she's spinning a sad story."

Linwing turned to him, offering a reassuring smile. "It's okay, Saborkris. I'll figure this out. I can handle it. Besides, she might not be completely wrong. If this Ry-tor is as dangerous as she says, maybe it's worth checking out."

Saborkris's fur bristled slightly, but he didn't argue. He had been with Linwing long enough to know that when she made up her mind, nothing would stop her. Still, a deep unease gnawed at him.

Linwing's wings fluttered lightly as she turned back to the Queen, who was now watching them with a calculating look in her eyes. Linwing nodded resolutely, "I'll help you."

The Queen's lips curled into a cruel smile. "Good. You'll be a valuable ally." She turned, her minions trailing behind her as they began to move deeper into the jungle.

Linwing took a final glance at Saborkris, her heart heavy but her resolve firm. "I'll be back soon," she called to him, before flying off to follow the Queen, her wings cutting gracefully through the air once more.

Saborkris stood there for a moment, watching her disappear into the trees. He was still uneasy, but he knew Linwing. She was strong, perhaps more than anyone could ever imagine. Still, this felt wrong. He couldn't shake the feeling that they were walking into something dangerous, something far darker than they realized.

But he had to trust her. For now.

The jungle whispered around him, the shadows stretching long as he waited, keeping watch.

Part 5:

The sky stretched out above them, vast and unbroken, as Linwing and the Mega Mosquito Queen flew side by side through the towering trees. The wind whipped past them, ruffling Linwing's feathers and making them sparkle in the sunlight. She reveled in the freedom of the flight, yet a part of her couldn't shake the feeling that something about this situation wasn't quite right.

The Mega Mosquito Queen, for her part, seemed perfectly at ease; almost too much at ease. She had a way of floating through the air, her wings gliding through the sky like an expert pilot, every movement controlled, every gesture precise. Linwing could barely keep the excitement from her voice as she spoke, her natural energy contagious.

"Thanks for trusting me," the Queen said suddenly, her voice a little softer than Linwing had expected. "It's not often someone just offers their help like that. I appreciate it. It's... rare."

Linwing tilted her head, "No problem at all! I help others whenever I can. It's what I do. Helping is what makes me... well, me." She gave a playful flap of her wings, soaring a bit higher, her heart light. "Plus, how could I say no to someone who looks so, well, *impressive* in the air?"

The Queen glanced at her, the edges of her lips curling into a tight, thin smile. She didn't seem entirely convinced by Linwing's compassion, but she didn't say anything. Instead, she moved her head slightly, watching Linwing with a keen interest.

"So, Linwing, tell me more about yourself. I've never heard of anyone like you before. A parrot with so much... *potential.* Where did you come from?" she asked.

Linwing didn't immediately answer, her sharp, eagle-like eyes narrowing with curiosity. "I've been around the jungle for a while. Been in a few scraps, helped out with a few battles. But I always try to keep things light. Life's too short to take it all seriously, right?" She chuckled, the sound light and carefree, but her gaze flickered back to the Queen, sensing the underlying tension in the conversation. "I've never heard of anyone like you either, honestly. I mean... you've got those wings, and those claws... who *are* you? What happened to you?"

The Queen glanced at Linwing again, her face betraying the slightest hint of annoyance, though she masked it with ease. "Oh, you know, the usual... life. Nothing too interesting, really. Just the way things go when you're trying to build something... meaningful."

Linwing raised an eyebrow, the corner of her beak turning up in a smile. "Sounds like you've got some stories to tell. But, hey, we all do, right?" She paused, then, with a mischievous glint in her eyes, she added, "Speaking of which, I've got a pretty fun story about me and Saborkris from the other day. You wouldn't believe how many trees he managed to knock over when he tripped over his own tail. He was *so* embarrassed!"

Linwing giggled, the lightheartedness of the story filling the air between them. Her wings flapped joyfully as she mimicked Saborkris's large, clumsy movements in the air. "And then, just when he thought no one saw, he tried to pretend like it was part of his grand plan! You should've seen his face when I told him I was *definitely* going to tell everyone about his 'tail-tumbling tactics.'"

For a moment, the Queen seemed to stiffen, her jaws clenching ever so slightly. But she quickly caught herself, forcing a tight chuckle to escape her lips. "That's... adorable," she said, her tone far too stiff to be sincere. "But I'm sure *he* didn't appreciate it much."

"Oh, he definitely didn't," Linwing said, laughing harder now, her voice almost musical. "But that's what makes it so fun! You've got to laugh at yourself sometimes, right? Even when you're the toughest one in the jungle, you've got to be able to look at the small stuff and just laugh."

The Queen nodded curtly, clearly losing interest in the topic but keeping her face carefully neutral. "Yes, laughter is important, I suppose."

Linwing's voice softened slightly, sensing the change in the Queen's demeanor. "It's kind of funny though. We all have our 'things,' right? I mean, Saborkris's got that big, tough guy act, but I know he's got a big heart underneath it all. I think that's what makes him so special. What about you? What's your thing?"

The Queen's expression darkened, the trace of amusement fading from her face entirely. She glanced at Linwing, her lips parting slightly as though she might say something. But then she paused, her eyes glaring with a calculating stare.

"There's something to be said for power," she said carefully, her voice now taking on a deeper, more measured tone. "You know, with your strength and your abilities, you could do so much more. You could be a force... a leader. You could join something greater, something that will give you more than just the jungle. Think of the possibilities."

Linwing blinked, surprised by the suggestion. "Join something? Like what?" Her voice held a hint of skepticism, though there was also a spark of interest in her eyes. She had always been someone who preferred to be alone, but the idea of being part of something... something bigger than herself, was tempting. After all, it had crossed her mind more than once that she might be able to do more with her special powers if she had the right companions by her side.

The Queen glanced at her, her expression unreadable. "A team. A formidable one. You've seen what you're capable of. Your fire, your wings, your strength. You could accomplish so much more if you weren't alone. Why not have someone by your side who shares your vision?"

Linwing's feathers rustled as she thought about it, the idea slowly taking root in her mind. "A team, huh?" She hesitated, her mind turning over the possibility. "I mean, that could be kind of cool, I guess. I've always kind of felt like there's more I could do; more I could give." She glanced at the Queen, her eyes narrowing slightly. "But who exactly are we talking about here? What kind of team?"

The Queen's eyes glinted with something darker, almost predatory. "A team that will change the world. You'll see. Join me, Linwing. With your skills, we could create something extraordinary. Together, we could have everything."

Linwing's wings fluttered again, uncertainty clouding her usually bright demeanor. She had always valued freedom, and the idea of being tied to someone else, no matter how important they were, felt strange to her. But the Queen's words had planted a seed, and Linwing couldn't help but wonder if this could be the next step for her.

"Well, I'm not saying yes just yet," Linwing replied, her voice a mix of intrigue and caution. "But I'm listening."

The Queen's lips curled into a satisfied smile. "Good. I think you'll find that this... opportunity will be worth your while. Be patient, and I'll show you."

As they continued flying together through the jungle, the landscape beneath them seemed to grow darker, the shadows stretching longer as the weight of the Queen's words lingered in the air. Linwing's thoughts were torn between the excitement of the unknown and the uneasy feeling that this might not be as simple as it seemed.

In the distance, the jungle whispered its secrets, and Linwing couldn't shake the feeling that something much bigger than her, than all of them - was about to unfold.

Part 6:

The air was thick with tension as the Mega Mosquito Queen and Linwing flew side by side. Above them, the sky was painted in shades of orange and pink, the last remnants of daylight fading into the twilight. The Queen's mind was elsewhere, her thoughts swirling in a quiet storm of dark calculations.

After this... after I finish what I need to do, I can definitely convince her. She has the capability, the potential. She's perfect for what I need. Together, we can accomplish more than either of us ever dreamed.

Her thoughts were interrupted when her piercing eyes caught sight of something below: a small, humble hut nestled in the trees.

Without a word, the Queen's wings beat harder, her body halting in midair as she floated over the clearing. Linwing, flying beside her, cocked her head, confused by the Queen's sudden stop.

"What's up?" Linwing asked, her voice still light and curious, though her eyes scanned the ground below, sensing something was off.

The Queen remained silent for a moment, her gaze fixed on the hut. She had expected to find Ry-tor here, but there was no sign of him. Instead, an older Velociraptor, bent with age, but with a fire still in his eyes, stepped out of the hut, His face was rugged, his expression one of wariness mixed with familiarity, as if he knew trouble was never too far away.

The Queen frowned. This wasn't who she had been expecting. It was Ry-tor's grandfather, the one who had raised him and had sheltered him. It was Ry-tor she had to deal with. But her plans hadn't been for this old Raptor.

Linwing, noticing the Queen's tense posture, floated closer, her curiosity growing. "Who's that?" she asked.

The Queen's voice was deceptively calm as she replied, her mind already working on a new plan. "That's someone who's been keeping an eye on Ry-tor. A Velociraptor who knows too much. He has information, and I'm going to get it out of him."

Linwing frowned, still not fully understanding. "What's his deal?"

The Queen ignored the question, her thoughts already turning to the next step. "It doesn't matter. We're here to get answers."

She paused, considering the situation. The hut in front of them was small, humble, and unassuming…but it had to be a place of secrets. And that old man? He might hold the key to finding Ry-tor.

Then, in a low voice, she turned to Linwing. "I need you to burn it down."

Linwing blinked, taken aback by the request. "Wait, what? The hut? Are you sure?"

The Queen's voice was firm and authoritative. "Yes, burn it. We'll burn it to show him we mean business. We can't afford to let anything - *or anyone* - stand in our way."

Linwing hesitated, a flicker of doubt crossing her face. But something about the Queen's presence; her authority, her unwavering certainty that compelled her to comply. The Queen wasn't just asking; she was demanding. Linwing, despite herself, found it hard to deny her.

"Okay…" Linwing said reluctantly, still uncertain but too caught up in the Queen's commanding energy to pull back.

Taking a deep breath, Linwing's fiery power surged within her. She inhaled sharply, then exhaled in a jet of flame, the fire heaving fiercely as it shot out from her beak and engulfed the hut in a giant, explosive burst. The flames demolished the hut and a column of smoke spiraled into the sky.

For a moment, the heat was unbearable, and the air was filled with the sounds of crackling wood and roaring fire. Ry-tor's grandfather was critically injured. He looked up, and his eyes widened when he saw the Mega Mosquito Queen, towering over him like a nightmare made flesh.

"Where is he?" the Queen growled, her voice a low, dangerous hum.

The old Raptor shook his head, panic rising in his chest. "Ry-tor? He's gone! You'll never find him!" His voice cracked as he tried to stand his ground, but the fear in his eyes was undeniable.

Linwing, hovering nearby, could barely keep her wings steady as she watched the exchange. This wasn't what she had expected, not…*this*. The old Raptor was terrified. He wasn't even fighting back.

"Tell me where he is," the Queen demanded again, her claws flexing as her wings flared out behind her. "I'm not asking anymore." Linwing's feathers ruffled, a sick feeling settling in her stomach. *This doesn't feel right.*

The Queen stepped forward, her form casting a long shadow over the old Raptor. Her eyes, once calculating, now burned with something far darker; something that Linwing had only seen in moments of battle.

"Please," the old Raptor begged, but his voice was barely a whisper as he looked up at the Queen. "I... I can't tell you…"

Before he could finish, the Queen's arm swung down in a brutal arc, swift as lightning, and she struck him with a force that made Linwing gasp. The old raptor's body went limp, his life extinguished in an instant.

Linwing froze in midair, her wings faltering as she watched. The scene before her felt like it was happening in slow motion, as if the world had briefly stopped turning. Her eyes were wide, her heart hammering in her chest.

The Queen stood over the old Raptor's crumpled body, her breath steady, her gaze cold and unflinching. "There," she said flatly. "You're no good to me."

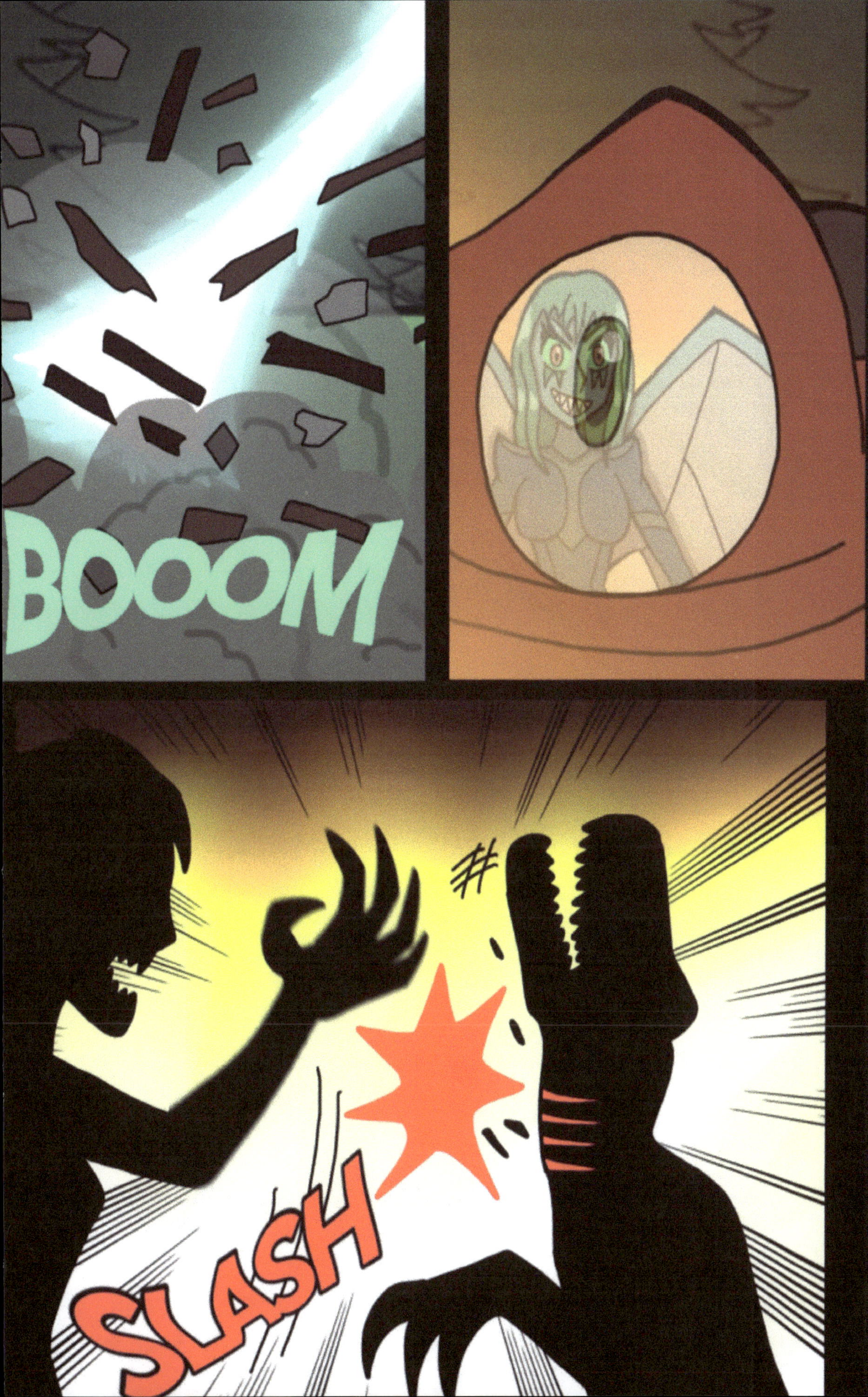
BOOOM
SLASH

Linwing was silent; her body trembling. "You... you killed him," she whispered, her voice barely audible. "He was just trying to protect his family. How could you do this!?"

The Queen turned to her, her expression shifting, softening just enough to mask the predator beneath. She bent down to Linwing's level. "Hey, don't worry about him. This is just the beginning. This is the *start* of something much bigger, something you'll be proud of. With your strength, you'll be unstoppable. And together, we can accomplish something special. Just think about it."

Then Linwing just flew off into the sky, as the queen was on the ground watching her fly off alone in the dimming sky. Linwing hovered in place, her mind racing, her body still frozen in shock. She had followed orders without question, had allowed herself to be drawn into this – *this* - moment.

But now, as the smoke from the hut rose in the distance and the storm clouds began to emerge above her, she couldn't shake the gnawing feeling that she had just taken her first step into a much darker world than she ever expected.

And it terrified her.

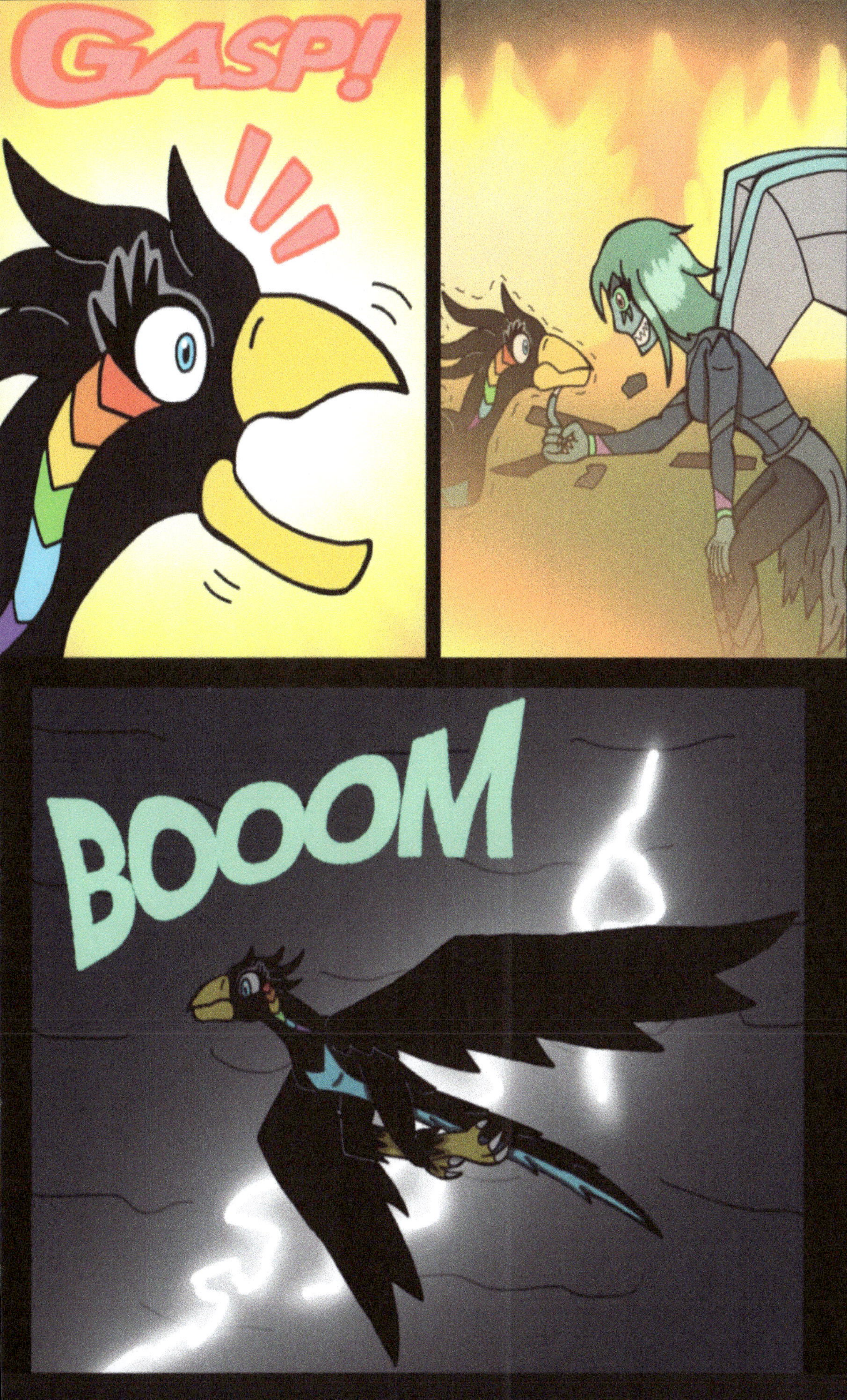
GASP!
BOOOM

Part 7:

The rain came down in torrents, a brutal downpour that lashed against the earth with an unrelenting fury. Linwing stood in a grass field a good distance away from the wreckage of the hut. She could smell the burnt wood and see the crumbling structure. It was now a reminder of the horrible decision she had just made.

Her breath was shallow, her wings heavy, and her heart was no longer light and carefree. *What did I do?* she thought, shaking her head as if trying to shake the terrible images from her mind. *I... I actually did that. I burned it down. I didn't know she would kill him.*

She should have listened to Saborkris. He'd warned her. He'd *always* warned her when something didn't sit right, but she hadn't listened. *I thought I was helping someone who needed it. I thought she was someone who needed help.* But now? Now she knew better. The Mega Mosquito Queen had used her; manipulated her like a puppet, and she had fallen for it.

How could I be so stupid? Linwing thought, her beak clenched tight in anger. *Saborkris... I can't even look him in the eye now. How do I even tell him what I did?*

With a piercing exhale, Linwing forced herself into motion. The rain only made it harder, but she couldn't stand there, staring at the wreckage, feeling sorry for herself. She needed space. She wanted time to think, to process what had just happened.

It started to downpour even harder. Each beat of her wings was a desperate attempt to outrun her thoughts, her feelings of guilt, shame, and rage. The wind whipped against her, but it couldn't cool the fire burning in her chest. She had always prided herself on helping others, on being there for people, but now she'd become part of something *awful.* She had *helped* the Queen; helped her destroy something... someone.

And it felt like she'd shattered a part of herself in the process.

Linwing's wings, usually so graceful, felt heavy as she flew aimlessly through the storm. The ground below blurred beneath the downpour, the grasslands turning into a haze of wet green. She was lost - not physically, but emotionally. She didn't want to think about the Queen. She didn't want to think about *anything*.

Suddenly, everything felt like it was crashing in on her. It felt like she was on the edge of losing herself. She let out a stabbing scream, the raw emotion spilling out of her. And then, without warning, it all snapped. The sadness that had weighed so heavily on her vanished in an instant, replaced by something far more powerful.

Anger. Pure rage. A fire ignited deep inside her, and she felt her body tremble with the force of it.

She didn't know where it came from, but it consumed her. Her vision sharpened, her mind cleared, but with only one singular focus: the Queen. She had made Linwing believe she was someone worthy of help. She had twisted Linwing's kindness and used it for her own gain. She had taken Linwing's trust and shattered it, turning her into a weapon of destruction. And Linwing wasn't going to let that slide.

Without thinking about what it might cost her; without thinking about the mistakes she had already made, she raised her head high. Her chest heaved with each breath, and the anger surged again. Her fire breath, normally controlled and used with caution, now burned with reckless intensity.

She opened her beak, and the flames erupted in an inferno, roaring through the air. The fire felt like it was coming from every inch of her body. She could feel it in her veins, in the way her heart pounded against her chest, the heat radiating from every muscle. It was an explosion of everything she had been holding in: the fear, the frustration, the sense of betrayal. It all came out in a single, explosive burst.

The ground beneath her feet began to smolder, the grass crackling as the fire lit the air around her. Linwing didn't care. All she could feel was the desire to unleash all of her fury on the Queen. She wanted to *make her pay* for what she had done.

Linwing's wings snapped open, and she shot into the sky with a burst of speed, breaking the sound barrier with a deafening crack that sent ripples through the air. The wind howled in her ears, but she didn't hear it. She didn't hear anything except the intense anger inside her.

Her body moved on instinct. She wasn't flying to get away, not anymore. She was flying to confront the Queen. To make her pay for what she had done. For what she had tricked Linwing into doing.

The wind whipped through her feathers, but it felt different now. The rain pounded against her like a million tiny needles, but she barely felt it. All Linwing could feel was the intense heat coursing through her, the inferno in her chest, and the purpose that had taken root in her heart. She was done with being manipulated. Done with feeling helpless. She was going to find the Queen, and when she did - nothing would stop her from making things right.

In the distance, she saw the familiar shape of the Mega Mosquito Queen's evil frame, her wings dark against the storm clouds. Linwing's eyes narrowed, her wings beating harder, faster. The Queen would pay. She would make sure of it.

As she neared her target, the anger inside her was too much to contain. She could feel the heat radiating from her body, and she knew that when she reached the Queen, it was going to explode.

Her wings sliced through the air as she closed in on the queen, and for the first time in a long time, Linwing felt no hesitation. There was only the fire inside her; and the anger that would burn everything in its path.

Part 8:

The Mega Mosquito Queen stood in the open, her figure dark and imposing against the stormy sky. Her wings twitched occasionally, sending small gusts of wind that swirled the leaves around her. She was waiting, calm and confident, for Linwing to come to her senses. She believed it was only a matter of time before the parrot would join her. She had manipulated Linwing, drawn her into the plan, and now she expected to persuade her to become an ally.

But something wasn't right.

One of the Queen's minions hissed sharply, alerting the Queen. She turned just in time to see a blur of blue and black streaking across the sky. Without warning, Linwing dove from the clouds faster than she had ever flown in her life, hitting the Queen with the force of a thunderbolt. The impact created a shockwave that knocked out the Queen's minions. Small rocks and branches were flung into the air as Linwing sent the Queen skidding across the ground, carving a deep trench in her path.

Linwing stood tall above the Queen, her wings thrashing furiously, her blue eyes flashing with fury.

"How dare you try to turn me into a tool of your evil plan!" Linwing shouted. "I won't be a part of this. I'll stop you!"

Lightheaded, the Queen slowly stood up and brushed dirt from her body. There was no trace of fear in her eyes, only disappointment.

"Linwing, you and I could've accomplished so much together," the Queen said, her voice smooth but cold. "But instead, you chose this. You've disappointed me, and I don't like anyone who disappoints me."

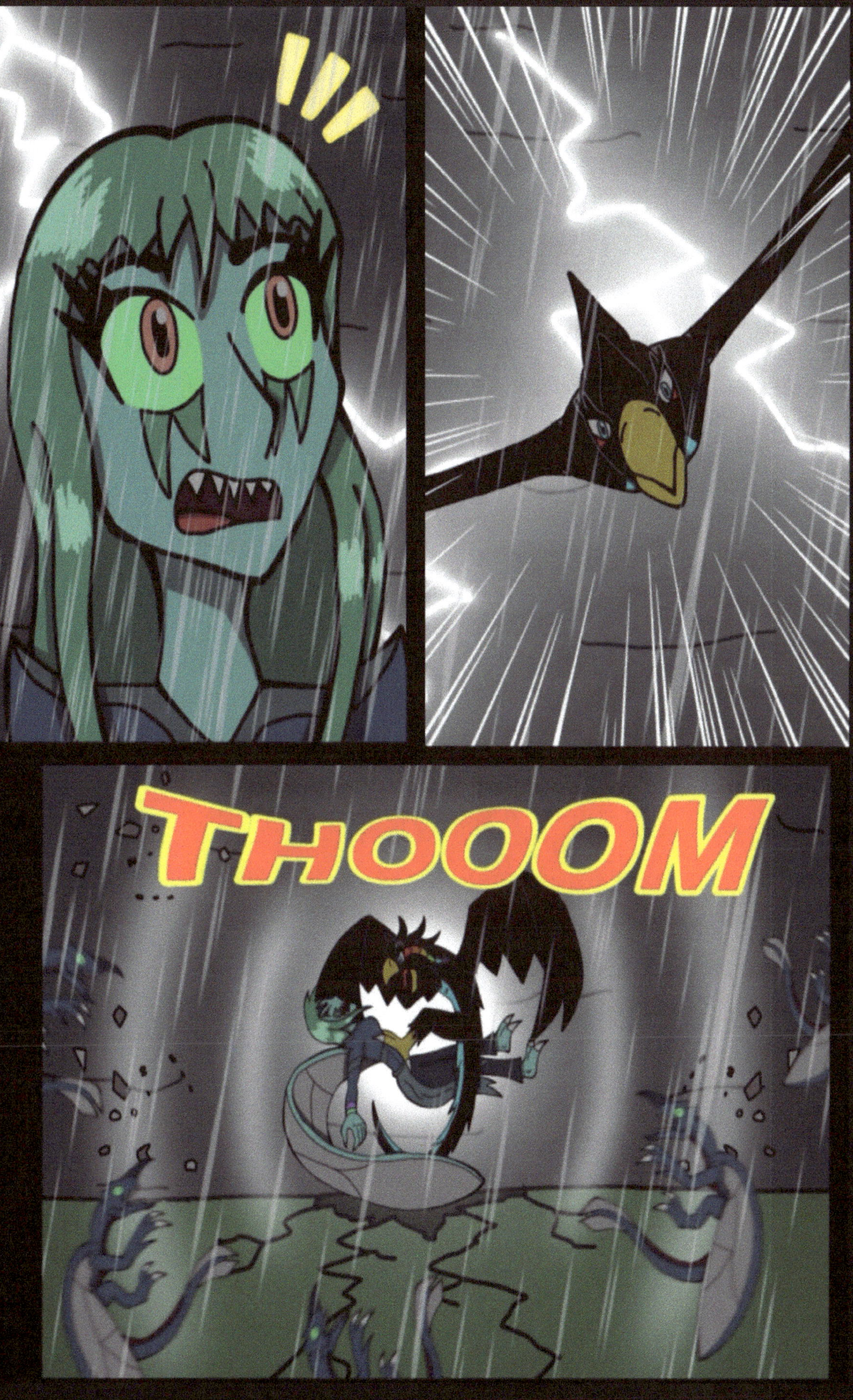
THOOOM

Linwing didn't waste a moment. With a quick flap of her wings, she lunged at the Queen, her tail whipping around to strike. The Queen managed to dodge the blow and kicked Linwing back with all her strength, sending the parrot soaring through the air.

The Queen wasn't done. She raised her hands and gave a swift command. Her minions, sensing the fight was on, scurried forward, leaping onto Linwing's back and biting down on her tail. The insects were half the size of her, but they were persistent, and Linwing growled in frustration.

These gnats are nothing compared to me, Linwing thought.

With a powerful shake of her wings, Linwing dislodged the minions. One of them clung to her tail, but she swung it up and down, slamming the minion hard into the ground. Another crawled up her back, but Linwing shook it off and stomped on it, crushing it beneath her talons.

The remaining minions charged, but Linwing was far too strong for them. She took a big deep breath and then unleashed her fire, sending a wave of flames over the charging creatures. The fire quickly consumed them, leaving only smoldering remains.

Linwing lifted her head, letting out a mighty roar, a battle cry that echoed through the jungle. The Mega Mosquito Queen watched her, assessing the situation, before taking flight herself.

"Let's see how you handle this," the Queen muttered, beating her wings and rising into the sky to meet Linwing in the air.

The two were soon locked in a fierce aerial battle. Linwing darted around the Queen, her movements fast and fluid, while the Queen retaliated with a barrage of razor-like stingers and sonic shrieks meant to disorient Linwing. But the parrot was too quick. Every time the Queen came close, Linwing would slip out of the way, her fire breath scorching the Queen's body with every hit.

Linwing pressed on, determined to take down the Queen. With one swift move, she launched a blast of fire directly at the Queen. The Queen was hit hard, plummeting toward the ground with terrifying speed. Linwing followed, diving after her, intent on finishing the fight.

Just before the Queen hit the ground, Linwing landed a kick directly to her stomach, making her hit the ground even harder. Linwing then threw the Queen like a rag doll across the grassland. Linwing rolled the Queen onto her back and pinned her down. The Queen struggled beneath Linwing's weight, but the parrot held her down with ease. Linwing's beak snapped forward, catching one of the Queen's wings. With a powerful jerk, she tore it free.

The Queen screamed in agony, her remaining wing fluttering weakly as she tried to push Linwing off.

The Queen's minions watched in stunned silence. They had never seen their leader so vulnerable.

Linwing stepped back, holding the Queen's torn wing in her beak as she stared down at the defeated Queen. The minions scattered, fear clearly evident in their eyes as they kept their distance from Linwing.

"Stay back!" Linwing warned, her voice low and commanding.

The Mega Mosquito Queen, still struggling to rise, turned her defiant gaze to Linwing.

"You… you think you've won?" the Queen hissed, her voice pained but laced with venom. "You're nothing but a parrot who got angry, who let your emotions control you. You helped me destroy Ry-tor's grandfather. How do you think he will feel when he finds out?"

Linwing's heart sank at the Queen's words. The weight of the Queen's accusation hit her harder than any blow. She had been manipulated. She had helped in something unforgivable.

The Queen snickered weakly, her voice barely audible. "You can't undo what you did, Linwing. You'll never, ever be able to change that."

The Mega Mosquito Minions, who had been watching in fear, suddenly surged forward to help her. As the minions grabbed her, they lifted the Queen into the air, her injured body still twitching in pain.

Linwing stood frozen, the fire of battle slowly fading from her. She glanced at the Queen one last time, her grip tightening around the wing still in her mouth. The Queen gave her a mocking, pained smile as her minions flew off into the distance, retreating into the clouds.

Linwing's heart raced as the storm raged around her, but all she could hear was the Queen's voice echoing in her mind. She had made a terrible mistake. She had been tricked, used. The question now was: could she live with the consequences?

Part 9:

The rain fell in heavy sheets, pounding against the earth like an endless drum. Linwing stood in the middle of it all drenched to the bone, her feathers soaked and clinging to her shaking body.

She turned, eyes haunted as they locked onto the flames still flickering in the distance. The trees were burning, their once proud branches now consumed by the fire she had unleashed. The damage was undeniable. *This is all my fault*, Linwing thought bitterly, the realization sinking deep into her heart. The smoke, the flames, the destruction…all of it was the consequence of her own decisions. She couldn't escape it.

Her body trembled, not from the cold, but from the surge of emotions threatening to drown her. She was no longer the joyful, spirited parrot who loved to fly without a care in the world. That part of her had been shattered, replaced by something darker; something excruciating. She had been manipulated. She had now caused harm to innocent lives. The weight of her actions pressed down on her like a boulder, and the guilt gnawed at her insides.

A soft sob escaped her beak, and Linwing clenched her jaw, trying to hold back the flood of tears. But they came anyway, streaming down her face, mixing with the rain. She was no longer the vibrant hero she had once been. She had failed herself, and worse, she had failed Saborkris. The one who had always been there for her. The one who believed in her when no one else did. How could she face him now?

I'm a monster, she thought, the words cutting deeper than any physical injury ever could.

She closed her eyes for a moment, taking a slow breath. The fury that had surged through her earlier was gone now, replaced by a deep sorrow. But the anger was still there, bubbling beneath the surface. It wasn't the kind of anger that burned hot and quick. This was the slow, smoldering kind; the kind that ate away at everything it touched.

She shook her head, trying to shake off the weight of it all. *I can't stay here,* she thought. *I need to face this. I need to tell Saborkris.*

Her wings spread wide, the feathers slick with rain, and with a powerful beat, she soared into the sky. The wind whipped around her, but she didn't care. She was numb to everything except the weight of her guilt, her regret. She flew with the storm now, pushed onward by something deep inside her that told her to go find him. To confess.

The flight back to the jungle felt like an eternity. Every beat of her wings carried her further from her mistake, but the distance didn't make the guilt fade. It followed her like a shadow. She could feel it weighing her down, each gust of wind feeling like a reminder of how badly she had messed up.

Finally, the familiar sight of the jungle came into view, the trees swaying gently in the storm's wake. It was peaceful here, a stark contrast to the chaos she had just left behind. But peace felt hollow. She felt hollow.

She found Saborkris near their usual meeting spot, his large figure visible even in the heavy rain. He looked up when he saw her, his amber eyes filled with concern. But as soon as their gazes locked, Linwing's resolve shattered. She didn't want to be strong anymore.

She dropped from the sky, landing in front of him with a heavy thud. Her legs trembled as she lost her balance, her wings dragging against the wet ground as she collapsed onto her knees. The dam inside her broke, and the tears came again, louder and more desperate this time.

Saborkris rushed to her side, his huge paws splashing in the rain as he knelt down beside her. "Linwing…" he said softly, his voice low and comforting. "What's wrong? What happened?"

"I - I've done something terrible," she choked out, her words coming in broken sobs as her heart was racing. "I… I thought I was helping. I thought I was doing the right thing. But I was wrong. I helped someone; someone who lied to me, who used me. I've made things worse… I don't know how to fix it."

Saborkris didn't hesitate. Without saying a word, he gently wrapped his large paws around her, pulling her close. He didn't say anything at first, but just held her, his warmth and strength enveloping her like a protective shield. Linwing tensed at first, not used to being this vulnerable, but slowly, she melted into his embrace. She sunk her face into his shoulder and let the tears fall freely, the weight of everything crumbling down on her all at once.

"I'm sorry," she whispered through the sobs. "I'm so sorry."

"You don't need to apologize to me, Linwing," Saborkris murmured, his voice steady and reassuring. "You're here now. That's what matters. You're not alone in this."

Linwing pulled away slightly, wiping at her eyes with her wing. She couldn't look at him, not yet. She felt so small, so broken. "But I failed you. You warned me. You told me to be careful, and I didn't listen. I made the wrong choice."

Saborkris's eyes softened as he looked down at her, his gaze full of understanding. "Linwing, we all make mistakes. Heck, I've made my share of them. You can't change the past, but you can change what happens next. You still have a chance to make things right. We'll figure it out together."

Linwing's heart ached at his words. How could he be so kind, so understanding, after everything that had happened? She had helped a villain. She had let her emotions get the best of her. And yet, Saborkris wasn't angry. He wasn't disappointed in her. He was here, comforting her when she felt like the world was crashing down around her.

"I don't deserve your forgiveness," Linwing whispered, her voice cracking.

"You don't have to deserve it," Saborkris said softly. "It's not about that. It's about who you are. And I know who you are. You're the one who always picks yourself back up, no matter how hard things get. And I'm here for you, no matter what."

Linwing looked up at him, her heart swelling with gratitude and guilt in equal measure. She had always been there for others, but now she was the one who needed help, who needed someone to lean on. And in this moment, she realized she wasn't as alone as she thought.

The storm raged on, but the air between them felt strangely still, as if the world had paused for just a moment. Linwing's wings were still heavy, her heart still burdened, but for the first time since everything had gone wrong, she felt a small glimmer of hope. Maybe, just maybe, there was still a way to make things right.

"I'll do better," Linwing said quietly, her voice steadying. "I'll make things right, for everyone."

Saborkris smiled, his large form protecting her. "I know you will."

Part 10:

The sun was just beginning to rise, casting a soft golden light over the still waters of the lake. The air was cool, the kind of crisp freshness that made everything feel new, like the start of a new chapter. Saborkris woke up early as usual. His paws padded softly against the damp earth as he approached the water to drink, the quiet ripple of the lake calming his thoughts.

But as he reached the edge, something caught his eye. To his right, by the water's edge, stood Linwing. She wasn't darting around the sky with her usual energy, her wings flapping with boundless excitement. No, today she stood motionless, her gaze fixed on her reflection in the water. Her usual playful sparkle was gone from her eyes, replaced by a dullness that seemed to mirror the overcast sky above. The breeze ruffled her feathers lightly, but she didn't seem to notice.

Saborkris's heart sank. He hadn't seen her like this in… well, ever. Linwing was always the light in every room, the one who could turn even the darkest of moments into something brighter with a single laugh. But now, there was only silence. His expression dropped, sadness creeping in as he walked over to her, his large paws making soft thuds on the ground. He didn't speak immediately, unsure of what to say.

Finally, he sat beside her, close enough that their shoulders almost touched. And they sat there, in complete silence, the only sound the soft ripple of the lake and the distant rustling of the trees in the wind. The stillness between them was heavy, thick with unspoken words.

Saborkris didn't mind the silence; sometimes, silence was enough. But this? This felt different. This was a silence born out of pain. He didn't need to ask what was wrong: he knew. It was the weight of everything Linwing had been through, the guilt of her actions, the doubts swirling in her mind. He just needed to figure out how to help her find herself again.

After a few minutes, he spoke, his deep voice breaking the stillness. "You know, Linwing… You're kind of like a firecracker."

Linwing didn't respond, still staring at the water, but Saborkris could see the tiniest twitch of her beak, like she might be holding back a smile.

"I mean it," he continued, his tone light but sincere. "You're the kind of friend who comes in with a bang, lighting up everything around you. You're full of life, of energy, of *flames*," he added with a chuckle, nudging her playfully with his shoulder.

A small laugh escaped her, though it was more out of habit than anything else. She glanced at him briefly, her eyes tired but grateful. "You always know how to make me laugh."

Saborkris grinned. "Hey, it's my job."

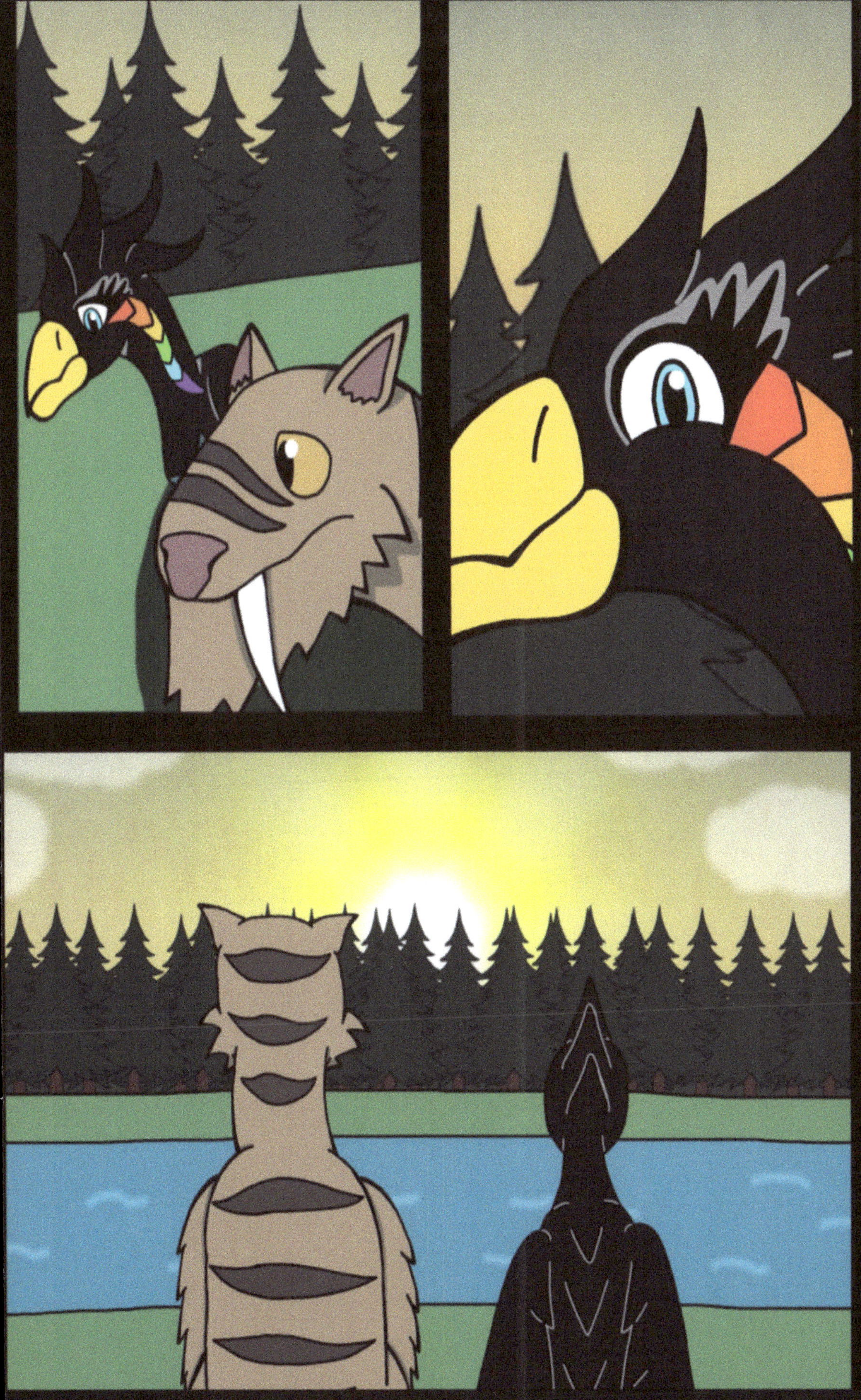

She smiled faintly, her gaze drifting back to the lake. The weight on her chest was still there, but the small spark of warmth from Saborkris's words gave her a moment of peace.

The two of them sat in silence again for a while, until Linwing finally spoke up, her voice quiet, almost uncertain.

"Saborkris, I've been thinking. About everything that happened." She hesitated for a long moment, the words catching in her throat. "I need to find Ry-tor."

Saborkris's head tilted in curiosity. "Ry-tor, the Velociraptor?"

Linwing nodded, a frown settling on her beak. "I... I need to tell him what happened. What I did. I have to explain myself. I need to make it right. I can't let the guilt eat me up like this."

Saborkris looked at her seriously, his amber eyes peering at her. He could see the resolve building inside her, but also the hesitation. It was like she wasn't sure if she could pull it off—or if she even deserved to.

"Are you sure about this?" he asked, his voice softer now. "You don't even know where to find him."

"I know," she said quietly. "But I have to try. I can't live with myself if I don't. I helped take his family away from him and I need to make it right."

Saborkris nodded slowly, his tail swishing thoughtfully behind him. "You're right. You do need to make it right. But you also need to understand that there might not be a simple 'fix.' Ry-tor might not want to hear you out. He might be angry. He might attack you."

Linwing flinched, her wings ruffling nervously. "I know," she whispered. "But I have to try."

Saborkris let out a deep breath. "I get it. I do. But don't go rushing into this, Linwing. You don't have to go alone. If you want, I'll come with you. We can find him together."

She turned her head to look at him, her eyes filled with gratitude. She opened her mouth to say something, but paused, realizing that Saborkris was right. She *could* try to make things right, but it wouldn't be easy. There were consequences to her actions, things she couldn't undo. And that scared her. But the more she thought about it, the more she realized she couldn't live with the shame of turning her back on it all.

She stood up slowly, stretching her wings out, the rain now a soft drizzle around her. She turned to Saborkris, offering a small smile. "Thank you," she said softly. "For always being there. For reminding me who I really am. I'll figure this out, this is something I have to do on my own."

Saborkris gave her an encouraging nod. "You're stronger than you think. And no matter what happens, you'll always have someone by your side."

Linwing nodded, her heart swelling with a mixture of sadness and hope. She was scared. Terrified, actually. But she knew she had to do this.

"I'll be back," she said, her voice a little steadier now. "I promise."

Saborkris gave her a reassuring smile. "I'll be right here. Just be safe."

With that, Linwing took a deep breath, spread her wings, and took off into the sky. Her heart was heavy, but her resolve was clear. She was going to find Ry-tor. She didn't know where to begin, or what she would say, but she couldn't run from this anymore.

As she soared through the sky, she felt the familiar weight of the wind against her wings, the feeling of freedom she had once taken for granted. And for the first time in what felt like ages, she felt a spark of hope. Maybe, just maybe, she could make things right. "I hope you can forgive me Ry-tor." She said to herself.

Epilogue:

The Mega Mosquito Queen stood tall, her gaze fixed on the horizon, her once-torn wing now fully regenerated. The wing, shattered and shredded in her last battle with Linwing, had been healed by her formidable powers, and now it spread out behind her, fully intact. Her mind, however, was anything but healed. The defeat, the humiliation, it still lingered like a bitter taste in her mouth. But she was not one to dwell on failure. No, she would rise again. Stronger. Smarter. More dangerous.

With a deep, unsettling breath, the Queen flexed her newly restored wing, feeling the strength return to her body. "I'll make them all regret this," she muttered to herself, the dark promise of revenge thick in her voice.

But as she turned her attention away from the wreckage of her past failures, her eyes locked onto something new; something unexpected. A city. It stood in the distance, sprawling, shining under the setting sun. Cars zooming by, tall buildings rising into the sky, people bustling in every direction. What struck her wasn't just the city's size or scope. It was the hum of life, the pulse of human technology. She had seen plenty of primitive civilizations before, but this? This was something else entirely. She could feel it in the air - the scent of progress, of advancement. *Real power.*

A sly grin spread across her face. "I've seen these creatures before," she thought. "But their technology... they've mastered the impossible. And I've got something they'll never expect."

Her sharp, predatory eyes flicked to her minions. The momentary distraction from her own thoughts dissolved, but the curiosity burned deeper. She noticed two figures standing on the outskirts of the city: Two men in lab coats talking secretively. They were discussing something with fervor, their gestures animated.

The Queen took a few steps closer, her keen senses picking up snippets of their conversation.

"Dr. Mowhawk, the prototype's ready," the man said, looking over a stack of papers and charts.

Dr. Mowhawk, the scientist, turned to face him. The Queen's eyes widened as she overheard his name. Dr. Mowhawk. A scientist and very possibly the sort of person who lived on the edge of madness, someone who bent science to his will rather than follow any moral compass. The type of individual who, perhaps like her, saw the world only as a tool to be reshaped, to be remade into something new.

Her lips curled into a malicious grin. This was the opportunity she'd been waiting for.

"What's this about prototypes?" she murmured to herself, gazing at him intently.

As she advanced closer, she noticed the unmistakable appearance of advanced technology in Dr. Mowhawk's hands. The devices were strange, glowing and almost alien-looking. They seemed to hum with a force of their own. There was no doubt in her mind now; these humans had tapped into something far beyond what the Queen had ever known. This could be the answer she was looking for. This could be her way to turn the tables once and for all.

Her thoughts swirled with possibilities as she approached Dr. Mowhawk, her wings folding with precision behind her. She needed to play this carefully; no more failures, no more mistakes. She could *use* him. She could *help* him. Together they could be unstoppable. They would bring chaos to this city, then to the world. She could feel the rush in her veins, the need to rise to the top.

The doctor was standing with his back to her, oblivious to the enormous threat closing in on him.

"Dr. Mowhawk, is that right?" The Queen called out, her voice smooth, commanding.

He whirled around in surprise, his eyes locking onto her with the shock of someone who had just encountered something he thought only existed in nightmares.

"Well, well," she purred, the grin never leaving her face, "I've been watching you and I think we could be of *great* help to each other."

Dr. Mowhawk looked at her, his mind working quickly, as though weighing the odds of this encounter. After a long moment, he smiled. "You're not from around here, are you? I don't know what you are, but you may be right."

The Queen stepped forward, her eyes glinting with malice. "I believe together, Dr. Mowhawk, we could accomplish far more than either of us could alone." She leaned in, her voice dropping to a whisper. "We could rule them all. We could shape this world however we see fit."

Dr. Mowhawk grinned, his eyes alight with dark possibilities. "I think I'll take you up on that offer."

And with that, an unholy alliance was formed. The Mega Mosquito Queen and Dr. Mowhawk, two forces of destruction, standing together in a world on the brink of technological evolution… and anarchy.

"Let's begin," she said, her wings unfurling as she turned toward the city, her mind already racing with plans. She could see it all now: The power, the fear, the control. *Everything* was within her reach.

The destruction was coming. And this time, no one would be able to stop it.

THE END

Published by
Five Stones Publishing
Rochester, New York

ISBN 978-1-945423-75-8
First Edition – November 3, 2025

Printed in the United States of America